Little Bo Peep
Can't Get
to Sleep

For my sister, Betty
(Don't tell Mom!)

Thank you, Paul, Gianna,
Annie, Elaine, and especially Caitlyn Dlouhy.
—E. D.

To Sharon
—H. W.

Atheneum Books for Young Readers
An imprint of Simon & Schuster Children's Publishing Division
1230 Avenue of the Americas, New York, New York 10020

Book design by Sonia Chaghatzbanian
The text of this book is set in Imperfect.
The illustrations for this book are rendered in oil paint.

Manufactured in China
First Edition
2 4 6 8 10 9 7 5 3 1
Library of Congress Cataloging-in-Publication Data
Dealey, Erin.
Little Bo Peep can't get to sleep / Erin Dealey ; illustrated by Hanako Wakiyama.—1st ed.
p.   cm.
Summary: An original nursery rhyme that relates how worried Little Bo Peep is about her lost sheep
and whether she should tell her parents they are gone, as well as which familiar characters she went to for help.
ISBN 0-689-84099-3
1. Nursery rhymes. 2. Children's poetry, American. [1. Nursery rhymes. 2. Characters in literature—Poetry.]
I. Title: Little Bo Peep cannot get to sleep. II. Wakiyama, Hanako, ill. III. Title.
PZ8 .3 .D3415Li 2005   2003022938

To Sophia—
Happy Reading!

Little Bo Peep
Can't Get
to Sleep

written by Erin Dealey

illustrated by
Hanako Wakiyama

All the Best,
Erin
Dealey

2005
Atheneum Books for Young Readers
New York London Toronto Sydney

Little Bo Peep can't get to sleep.
She kicked her blankets in a heap.
"Try counting sheep," her mother said,
but Bo Peep lay awake instead.

Peep's tummy hurt; her head ached, too.

She wasn't sure just what to do.

She couldn't count her sheep, you see.

She didn't know where they could be.

She'd counted them in the meadow that day,

just before they ran away.

Then Little Boy Blue went and blasted his horn,

to scare the cows away from the corn.

The cows didn't budge. They were too full.

But the sheep were frightened right out of their wool!

"My sheep!" cried Peep to her brother, Blue.

Boy Blue replied, "What did *I* do?"

She'd asked the Farmer in the Dell,

and Jack and Jill up by the well.

No one had seen her missing sheep.

A wolf might get them! worried Peep.

Humpty Dumpty climbed his wall.

"Careful!" Peep said. "Please don't fall!"

"I see some pigs," he said with a smile.

"Go home. I'll stay and look for a while."

Peep met a troll along the way.

"Who dares to cross my bridge today?"

"Mr. Troll, have you seen my sheep?"

"Only goats,"
he snarled at Peep.

"Don't tell Mom," warned Little Boy Blue.

"You'll be in trouble if you do."

Peep said, "My flock will be home soon."

Blue laughed, "When cows jump over the moon!"

Dad tucked Peep in with a good-night kiss.

"It's past your bedtime, little miss."

She had to tell them about her sheep.

"Mommy? Dad?" began Bo Peep.

"A giant's underneath my bed!"
was the tale she told instead.
"I think he slid down Jack's beanstalk!"
"Hush," said Dad, "that's only talk."

"Good night," said Daddy with a yawn.

Peep worried that her sheep were gone.

"Close your eyes, my sleepy daughter."

"Please," Peep asked, "may I have some water?"

She whispered to the rising moon,
"I'll run away with the dish and the spoon!
Hey, diddle diddle—what should I do?
Tell Mom and Dad or listen to Blue?"

Moon gave a wink as if to say,

Your sheep are safely home to stay.

And Peep looked down to see her flock,
as Humpty ambled down the block.

Still, Little Bo Peep felt very lost.

Instead of sleeping, she turned and tossed.

"Mommy, rub my back?" she asked.

"I'm sure to fall asleep at last."

Mommy rubbed until it seemed
Bo Peep slept; Bo Peep dreamed.
But as Mom tiptoed from Peep's bed,
"I lost my sheep," a little voice said.

"They're home again. Moon told me so.
I just wanted you to know."
Peep felt better. "Are you mad?"
"Next time tell us sooner," said Dad.

Moon shined brightly on the town,

where Wee Willie Winkie ran up and down.

Little Boy Blue was fast asleep,

and Peep could finally count her sheep.

She didn't hear the Fiddler Cat's tune,
nor see the cows jump over the moon,
for Little Bo Peep was soon asleep
without a worry, without a peep.